To: _____

From: _____

Pearls of Wisdom

By Barbara K. Daly

Copyright © 2024 by Barbara K. Daly

All rights reserved. No part of this book may be reproduced or transmitted in any form or by any means, electronic or mechanical, including photocopying, recording, or by any information storage and retrieval system, without permission in writing from the copyright owner.

Published by
Barbara K. Daly
website address: www.BarbaraKDaly.com

ISBN: 978-1-7369730-6-6 Hardback

Author's Note

In March 2020, the world changed and realized that it was closing down because of Covid. As the weight of those times became clearer, in May, I started an email called, "Monday Musings." I wanted a way to connect with my extended family, my friends and clients, so I chose to create an email that I would send out weekly on Monday mornings. I wanted to begin each email with a positive and thoughtful quote. I never tried to "preach" but give my readers seeds to develop their own thoughts.

As an advisor at Sotheby's International Realty, I then added bits of real estate news, sometimes highlighting a local listing and other times, a listing somewhere throughout the world.

After a year of sending out the weekly emails, the world began to reopen. I then decided to then make it a Monthly Musing. The response I received was surprising. I hadn't realized the effect that a consistent Monday positive message was having on so many people and how many enjoyed that positive thought to start their week.

The Monday Musings continue today. Here are a just a few of the thoughts that I have previously shared. Every week, I get feedback from the recipients how a particular quote affected them personally. They won't always affect you every week but hopefully they will give you additional food for thought and how you approach each day and your life.

The book was written not to read pages consecutively, but to spark an inspiration by simply opening the book to whatever page and that would be your thought for the day.

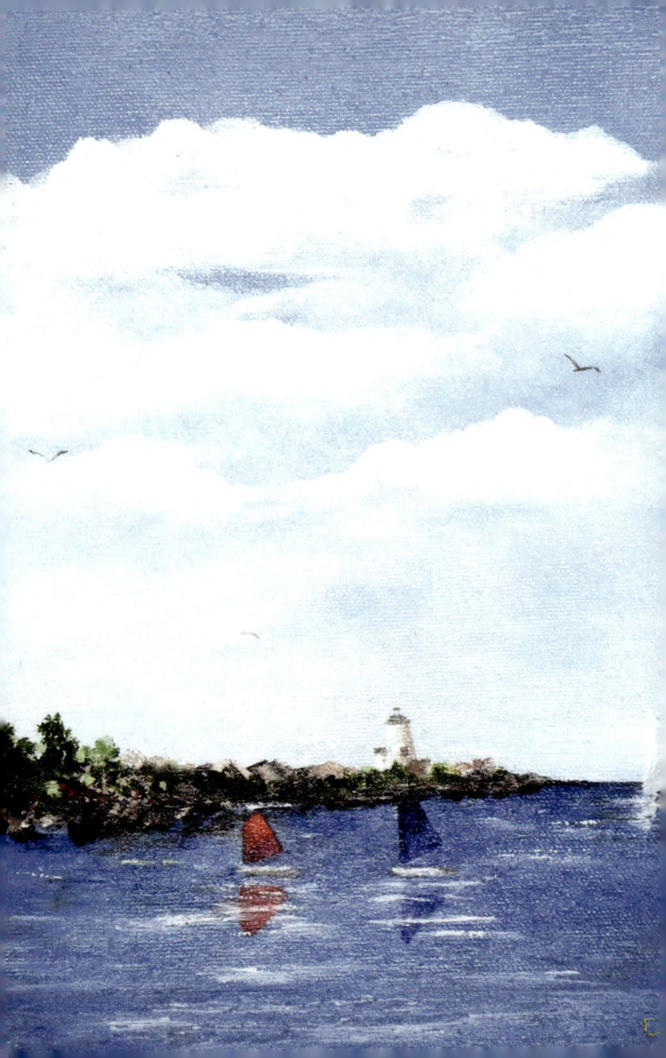

"There are two ways to live. You can live as if nothing is a miracle. You can live as if everything is a miracle."

~Albert Einstein

"Train your mind to see the good in everything. Positivity is a choice. The happiness of your life depends on the quality of your thoughts."

~Unknown

"When you rise in the morning, think of what privilege it is to be alive— To think, to enjoy, to love."

~Marcus Aurelius

*"Don't be pushed around
by your fears in your mind.
Be led by the dreams
in your heart."*

~Roy T. Bennett

"The day I stop giving is the day I stop receiving."

~Unknown

"But I know, somehow, that only when it is dark enough can you see the stars."

~Martin Luther King Jr.

"Worry does not take away tomorrow's troubles, it takes away tomorrow's peace."

~Unknown

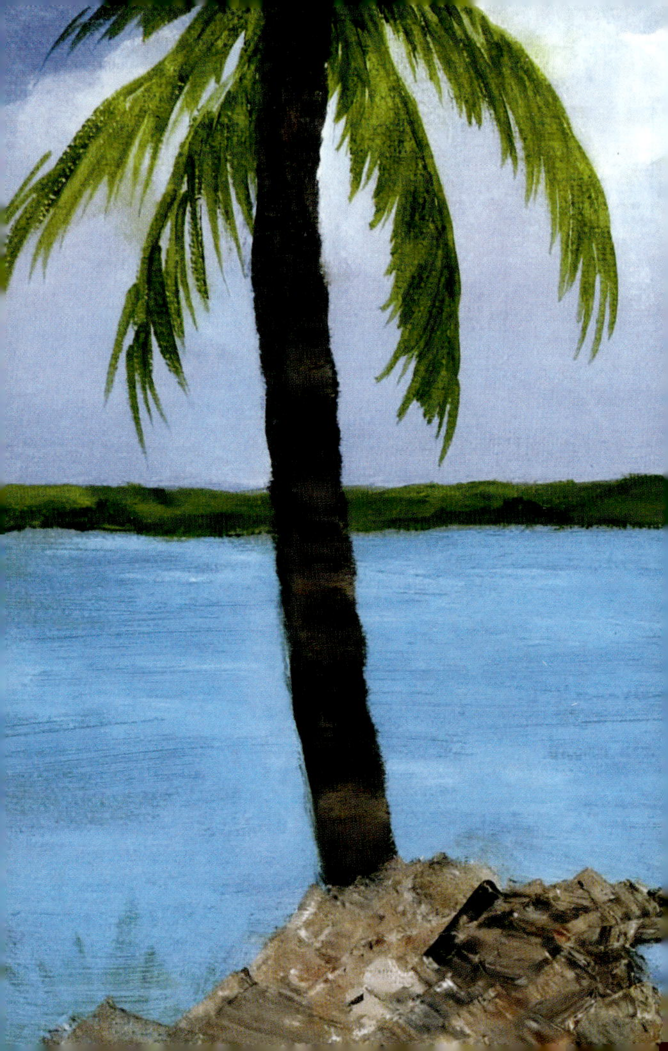

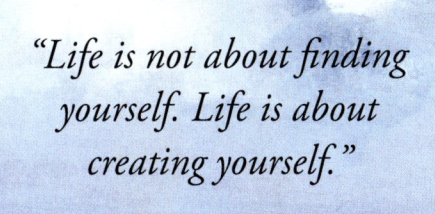

"Life is not about finding yourself. Life is about creating yourself."

~George Bernard Shaw

"It is during our darkest moments that we must focus to see the light."

~Aristotle

*"Let your Life
be your message."*

~Mahatma Gandhi

*"Success is not final:
failure is not fatal:
It is the courage to
continue that counts."*

~Winston Churchill

"A winner is a dreamer who never gives up."

~Nelson Mandela

"So often in life things that you regard as an impediment, turn out to be great good fortune."

~Ruth Bader Ginsberg

"A diamond is just a chunk of coal that did well under pressure."

~Henry Kissinger

"With the new day comes new strength and new thoughts."

~Eleanor Roosevelt

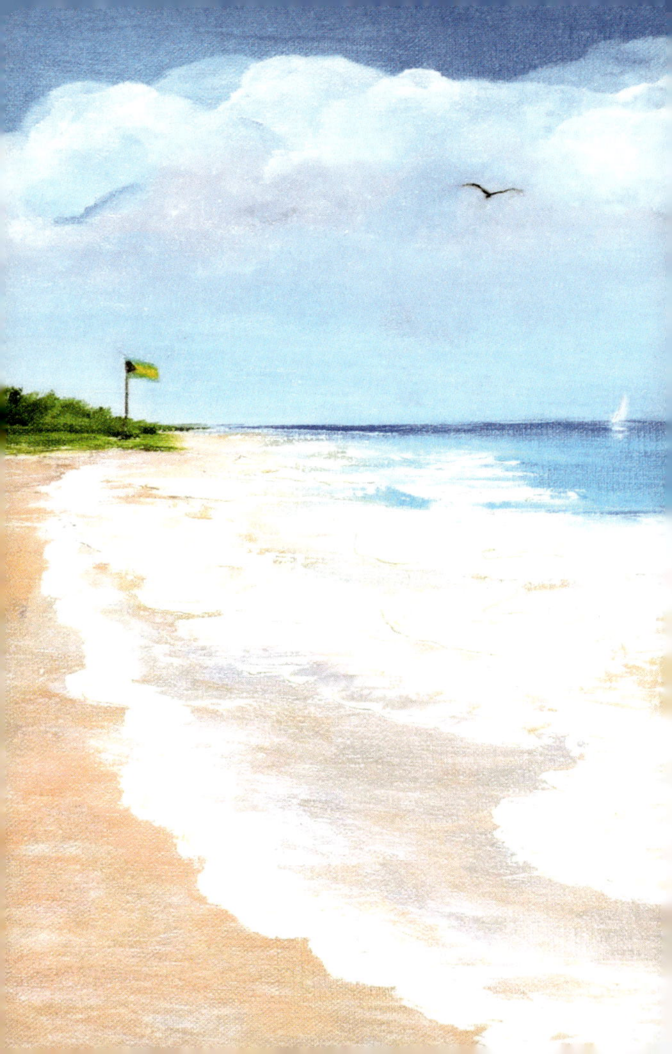

"The first step towards getting somewhere is to decide you're not going to stay where you are."

~J.P. Morgan

"Be thankful for what you have; you'll end up having more. If you concentrate on what you don't have, you will never have enough."

~Oprah Winfrey

*"Hope smiles from
the threshold of the year
to come, whispering,
"It will be happier."*

~Alfred Lord Tennyson

*"Darkness cannot
drive out darkness:
only light can do that.
Hate cannot drive out hate:
only love can do that."*

~Martin Luther King, Jr.

"Today is the first of a 365 page book. Write a good one!"

~Brad Paisley

"Wherever you go, no matter what the weather, always bring your own sunshine."

~Anthony J. D'Angelo

"In the end, it's not the years in your life that counts. It's the life in your years."

~Abraham Lincoln

*"Be the reason someone smiles.
Be the reason someone feels
loved and believe in the
goodness of people."*

~Roy T. Bennett

"May your heart be light and happy, may your smile be big and wide, and may your pockets always have a coin or two inside."

~Irish proverb

"A tulip doesn't strive to impress anyone, it doesn't struggle to be different than a rose. It doesn't have to. It is different. And there's room in the garden for every flower."

~Marianne Williamson

"Once you replace negative thoughts with positive ones, you'll start having positive results."

~Willie Nelson

"We are what we repeatedly do. Excellence, then, is not an act but a habit."

~Aristotle

*"Failure is not the
opposite of success:
it's part of success,*

*If your dreams don't scare you,
they are too small,*

*Believe you can and you're
halfway there."*

~Hope Perlman

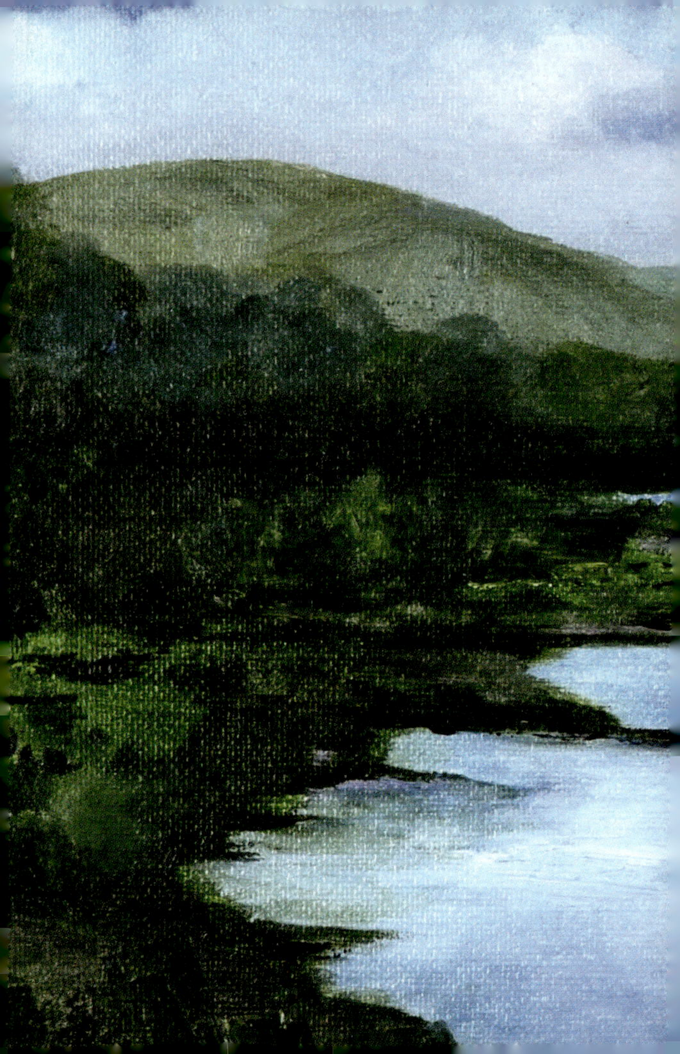

"*Someone out there feels better because you exist.*"

-Unknown

"Happiness is a choice, not a result. Nothing will make you happy until you choose to be happy."

~Ralph Marston

"A good life is when you assume nothing, do more, smile often, dream big, laugh a lot and realize how blessed you are for what you have."

~Zig Ziglar

"Luck is what happens when preparation meets opportunity."

~Lucius Annaeus Seneca
(Roman Philosopher)

*"It is not in the stars
to hold our destiny,
but in ourselves."*

~William Shakespeare

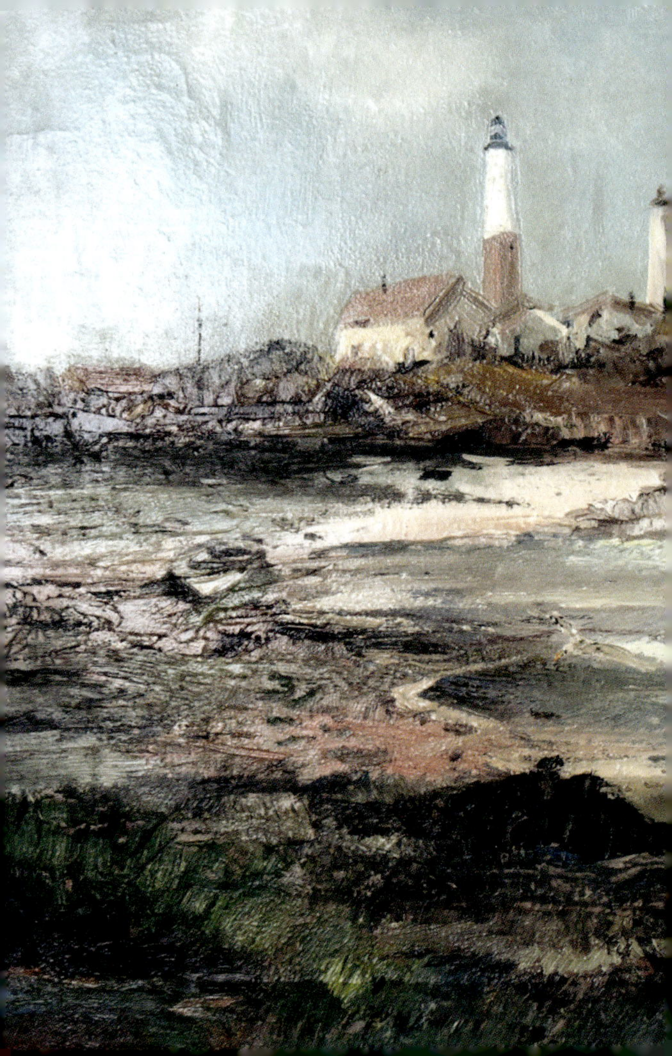

"Be yourself. Everyone else is already taken."

~Oscar Wilde

*"The golden opportunity you
are seeking is in yourself.
It is not in your environment;
it is not in luck or chance,
or help of others;
it is in yourself alone."*

~Dr. Orison Swett Marden

"Don't ever save anything for a special occasion, everyday of your life is a special occasion! Carpe Diem!"

~Thomas S. Monson

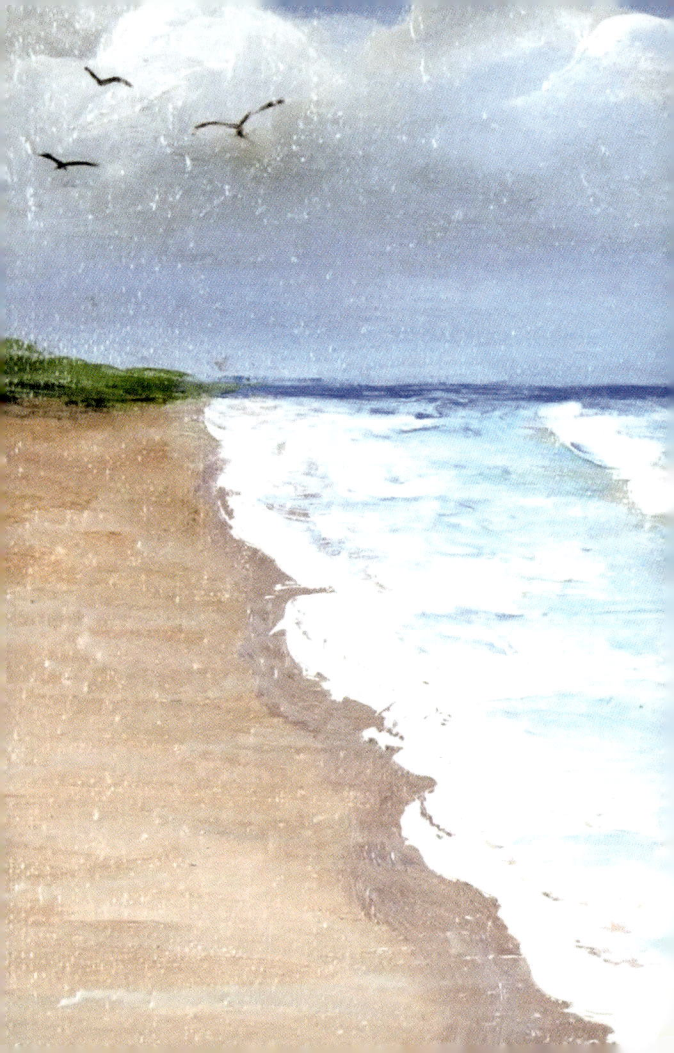

"There is never a night or a problem that could defeat a sunrise or hope."

~Bernard Williams

"Never put the key to your happiness in someone else's pocket."

~Unknown

"If my mind can conceive it and my heart can believe it—then I can achieve it."

~Muhammed Ali

"Because that's what kindness is, it's not doing something for someone else because they can't but because you can."

~Andrew Iskander

*"The best part about life?
Every morning you have a
new opportunity to become a
happier version of yourself."*

~Unknown

"Peace is not the absence of conflict, it is the ability to handle conflict by peaceful means."

~President Ronald Reagan

*"Always remember:
Grapes must be crushed to make wine.
Diamonds form under pressure.
Olives are pressed to release oil.
Seeds grow in darkness.
Whenever you feel crushed,
under pressure, or in darkness,
you are in a powerful place
of transformation."*

~Lalah Delia

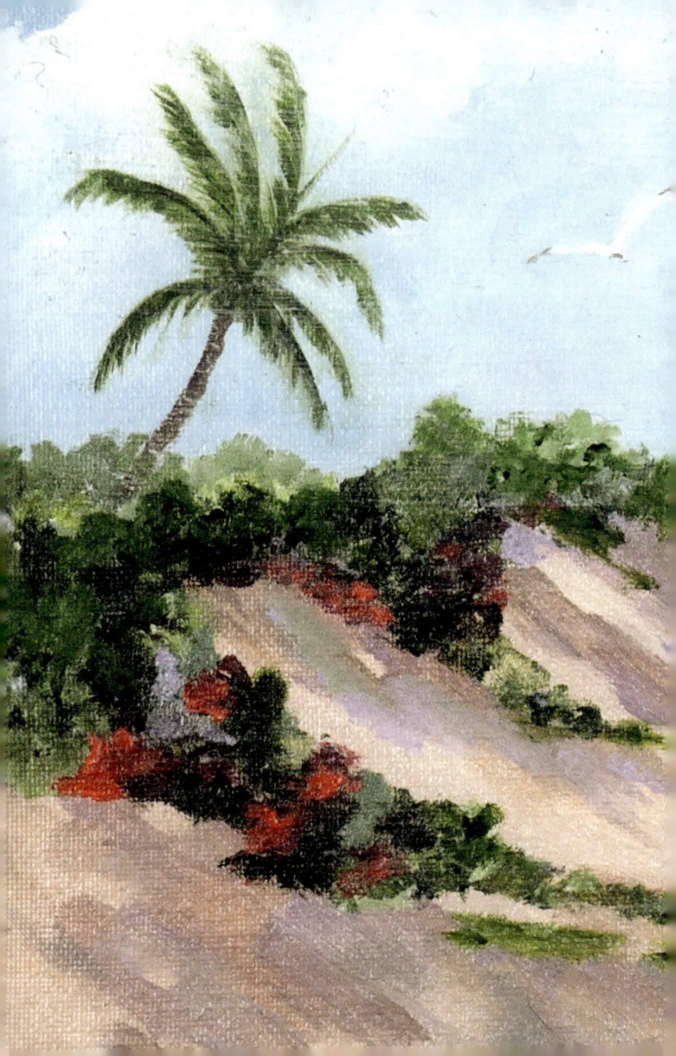

"No one can go back and start a new beginning, but anyone can start today and make a new ending."

~Maria Robinson

"By prevailing over all obstacles and distraction one may unfailingly arrive at his chosen goal or destination."

~Christopher Columbus

"The best things in life are free: hugs, smiles, friends, kisses, family, sleep, love, laughter, and good memories."

~Unknown

*"Stay positive!
The only difference between
a good day and a bad day
is your attitude."*

~Dennis S. Brown

"There are no secrets to success. It is a result of preparation, hard work, and learning from failure."

~Secretary Colin Powell

"Happiness – Everyone wants happiness, no one wants pain. But, you can't have a rainbow without the rain."

~Ingmar Bergman

*"Be strong, but not rude.
Be kind, but not weak.
Be humble, but not timid.
Be proud, but not arrogant."*

~Zig Zigler

"You are the sum total of everything you've ever seen, heard, eaten, smelled, been told, forgot — it's all there. Everything influences each of us, and because of that I try to make sure that my experiences are positive."

~Maya Angelou

"The more you feed your mind with positive thoughts, the more amazing things take root and happen. This is because you attract what you think about most."

~Unknown

*"Everybody is a genius.
But if you judge a fish by
its ability to climb a tree,*

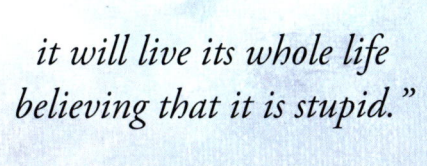

it will live its whole life believing that it is stupid."

~Albert Einstein

"Being positive in a negative situation is not naïve, it's leadership."

~Ralph Marston

"A society grows great when old men plant trees whose shade they know they shall never sit in."

~Greek Proverb

"Friends are the flowers in the garden of life; beginning with a seed of trust, nurtured with laughter and tears, growing into loyalty and love."

~Proverbs

"If you throw a stone into a pool, the ripples go on spreading outwards. A big stone can cause waves, but even the smallest pebble changed the whole pattern of the water. Our daily actions are like those ripples, each one makes a difference, even the smallest."

~Queen Elizabeth II

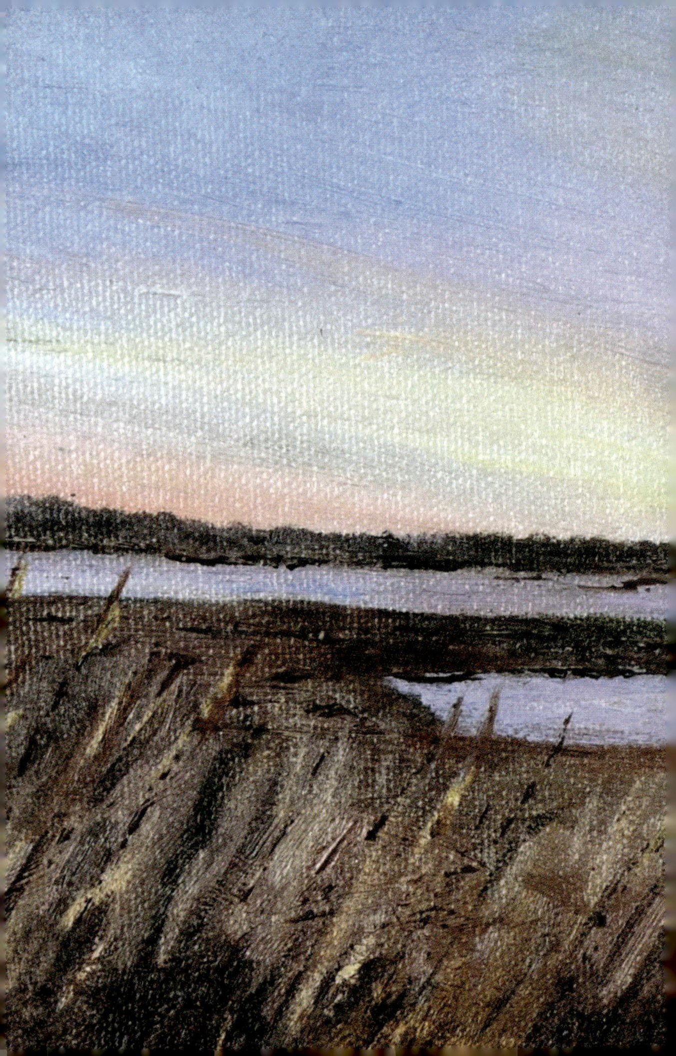

"Those who bring sunshine to the lives of others cannot keep it from themselves."

~J.M. Barrie

"Helping one person might not change the world. But it could change the world for one person."

~Anonymous

"The challenges you face introduce you to your strengths."

~Epictetus

"When you talk, you are only repeating what you already know. But if you listen, you may learn something new."

~Dalai Lama

"Our greatest glory is not in never failing, but in rising everytime we fail."

~Confucius

"Integrity is doing the right thing, even when no one is watching."

~C.S. Lewis

"People may not remember exactly what you did or what you said, but, they will always remember how you made them feel."

~Maya Angelou

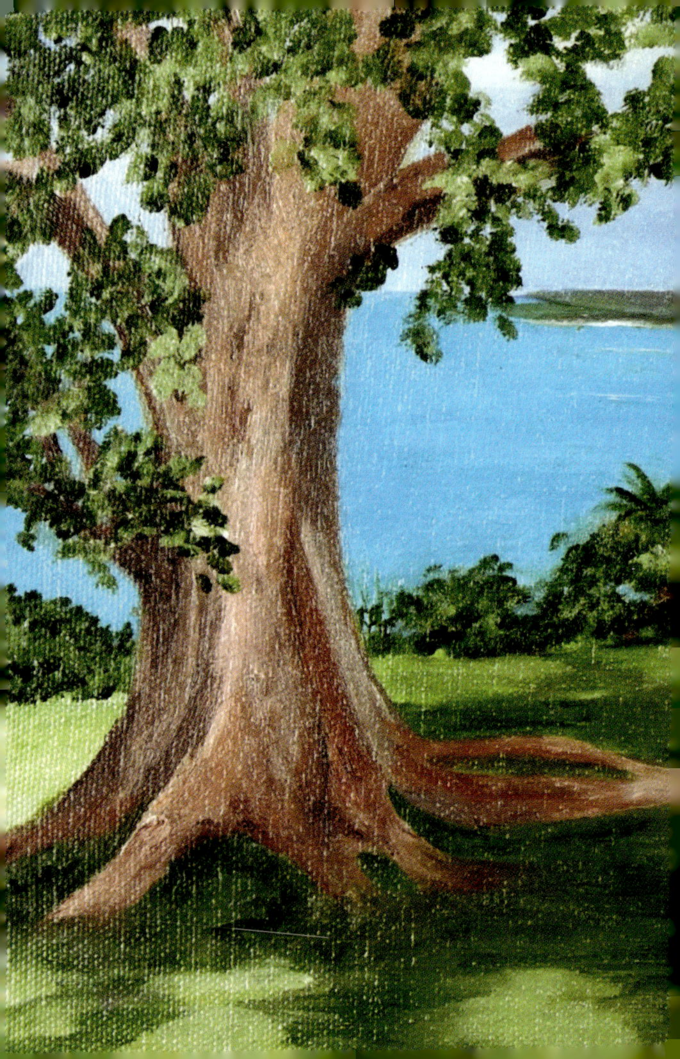

"Just as the acorn contains the mighty oak tree, the self has everything it needs to fulfill its destiny"

~Derek Rydall

*"I never lose.
I either win or learn."*

~Nelson Mandela

"A man is great not because he failed: a man is great because failure hasn't stopped him."

~Confuscius

*"Take chances, make mistakes.
That's how you grow.
Pain nourishes your courage.
You have to fail in order to
practice being brave."*

~Mary Tyler Moore

"Carry out a random act of kindness, with no expectation of reward, safe in the knowledge that one day someone might do the same for you."

~Princess Diana

"The gap between the life you want and the life you are living is called mindset, focus and consistency."

~Unknown

"You don't have to be great to start, but you have to start to be great."

~Zig Ziglar

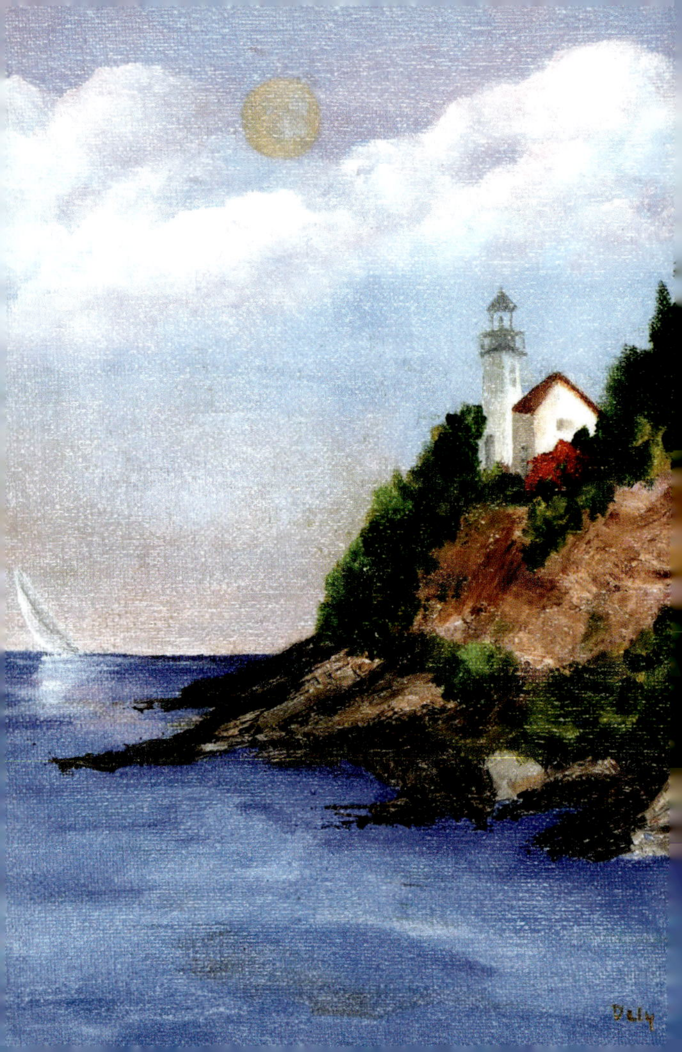
Daly

"I can't change the direction of the wind, but I can adjust the sails to always reach my destination."

~Jimmy Buffett

"Look for something positive in each day, even if some days you have to look a little harder. A positive mind will give you a happier life."

~Unknown

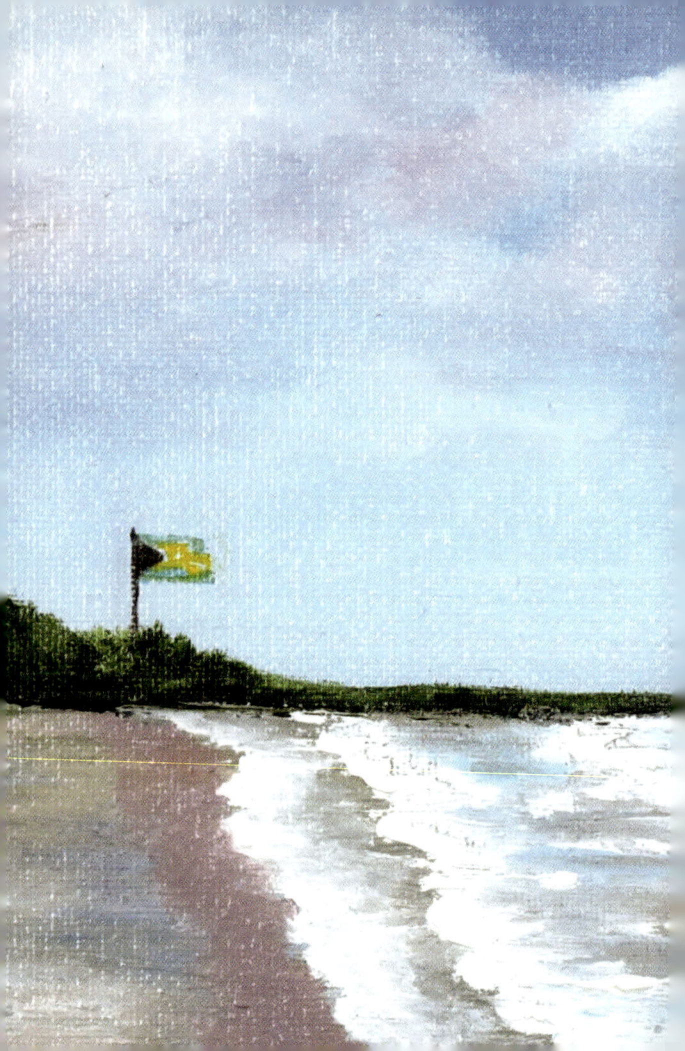

*"As we express gratitude,
we must never forget that
the highest appreciation is
not to utter the words,
but to live by them."*

~President John F. Kennedy

*"To the world,
you may be one person,
but to one person,
you may be the world."*

~Dr. Seuss

*"Every day may not be good,
but there's something good
in every day."*

~Alice Morse Earle

"Blessed is the season which engages the whole world in a conspiracy of love."

~Hamilton Wright Mabie

"Stay away from negative people. They have a problem for every solution."

~Albert Einstein

"Judge me not on the color of my skin, but by the content of my character."

~Martin Luther King, Jr.
Taken from his speech,
"I have a Dream."

*"The only way to
achieve the impossible
is to believe it is possible."*

~Charles Kingsleigh, "Alice's" father in
Lewis Carroll's Alices Adventures
in Wonderland

"Success is not for the chosen few, but for the few who choose it."

~Unknown

*"If you are positive,
you'll see opportunities
instead of obstacles."*

~Confucius

*"Never regret a day in your life.
Good days give happiness.
Bad days give experiences.
The worst day give lessons.
And the best give memories."*

~Dr. Sukhraj Ghillon

"Your smile is your logo, your personality is your business card, how you leave others feeling after an experience with you is your trademark."

~Jay Danzie

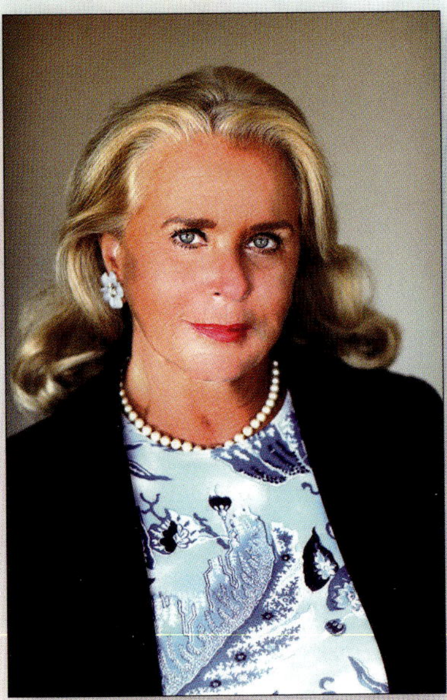

About the Author

Barbara Daly has, through the course of her life, been an interior designer, realtor, painter and mother, now a grandmother. This book is a broader reflection of the thoughts and motivations that allowed her to work and achieve her goals in these areas. Born in Wisconsin, Barbara spent her formative years in Coral Gables, Florida. Seeking a career in interior design, she attended the Parsons School of Design in New York City. Building a business there, she met her husband, John, and a few years on, moved to Connecticut. The Dalys had two children and in 1977 moved to Greenwich, Connecticut, where they live to this day.

While raising her two children, she was and continues to be involved in numerous community and charitable organizations. It was also at this time she discovered her talent and passion for painting and has done so not only in Greenwich, but all over Europe, The Bahamas and the Caribbean. Barbara has been in the real estate business for over 25 years with Sotheby's International Realty.

Barbara is also currently a member of the Greenwich Association of Realtors, Greenwich Multiple Listing Service, Connecticut Association of Realtors and National Association of Realtors.

Barbara is committed to giving back to the community in which she lives and works. She has taken part in fundraising for the Greenwich Historical Society, Greenwich Hospital and the Bruce Museum. She is a past president of the local garden club and is currently focused on Neighbor to Neighbor Greenwich, a charitable organization that provides food, clothing and basic living essentials to those in need.

Acknowledgements

Because of the love and support of my husband of 58 years, the world has been my oyster. He has let me be me. Never restricting me or my thoughts but always encouraging me. He always knew I had to fly and I was safe in the knowledge that my anchor was always there.

Family life has been very important to me. My children, John and Cristina, and now my grandchildren, Caroline and Jack, are a constant inspiration and source of never ending love. They have all been an integral part of this book.

My friends have always been "family we choose". In particular, Karen has been my friend for over 50 years. Our families relationship have been a constant reminder what friendship means. My west coast gal pals, Sharon and Anne, and my Florida/Nantucket pal, BH, are always a phone call away. When we do get together, it seems like no time or distance has come between us. Donna, my friend from high school, and I have painted together all over the world. My six "Sipstas" (Cindy, Darrah, Jackie, Jeannette, Kimberly and Shelly) are without question, six ladies I love, admire and respect. Indeed, we have a unique sisterhood.

I would be remiss in not acknowledging my Sotheby's International Realty family and all they have given me, both professionally and personally.

All of the above people have been an integral part of my journey.

My sincerest thanks to Darlene and Dan Swanson of Van-garde Imagery, an invaluable book design team who always anticipated my vision for this project. As well, great thanks to Phil Nanzetta of Signature Book Printing, whose responsiveness and skill made this process seamless.